This edition is published by Derrydale Books,
a division of Crown Publishers, inc.
by arrangement with Award Publications Limited

abcdefgh

Printed in Belgium

Enid Blyton

Hoo Hoo the Owl

Illustrated by
RENE CLOKE

DERRYDALE BOOKS
NEW YORK

HOO HOO THE OWL

Hoo Hoo the Owl was very hungry. He hadn't caught a mouse or a rabbit for a week, though he had tried hard every night. Whatever should he do?

He sat in his
hollow tree
and thought
hard.
Then a wonderful
idea came to him.

"I will give a party," he said to
himself. "I will ask Whiskers the Mouse,
Tailer the Rat, Soft Ears the Rabbit,
Singer the Nightingale, Mowdie the Mole
and Frisky the Squirrel.
Ha ha, Hoo Hoo!"

So he sent out his invitations, and this
is what the cards said:

Hoo hoo the Owl
invites
Whiskers the Mouse
to a party
on the next full moon
night in the
Hollow Tree.

He sent the cards, each with the name of
the person written on it, to Whiskers,
Tailer, Soft Ears, Singer, Mowdie and
Frisky. Then he waited for the answers.

Whiskers the Mouse was
delighted. He had never
been to a party in his life.
So he accepted gratefully.

Tailer the Rat was always hungry, and
the thought of a party made him joyful.
He thought that he would get there early
and eat a lot.
So he accepted too.

Soft Ears the Rabbit read his invitation
over and over again, very proudly. He had
only once been to a party, and it had been
so lovely that he had always longed to go
to another. So he accepted the invitation
too, and wrote a neat little answer.

Singer the Nightingale felt quite certain that she had been invited because of her lovely voice.

"I expect they will ask me to sing," she thought. "That will be nice, for they will all praise my beautiful voice."

So she accepted too, and sent her answer along that same day.

Mowdie the Mole had been to hundreds and
hundreds of parties, and he felt certain
that he had another one on the same night.
But when he looked in his notebook to see,
he found that he hadn't.

So he decided
that he would go,
and he scribbled an
answer at once.

Frisky the Squirrel
read Hoo Hoo's card
carefully.
Then he read it
again.
Then he read it
for a third time.

He didn't like
Hoo Hoo, and he
felt quite certain
that Hoo Hoo
didn't like him.

Why, then,
had he been asked
to Hoo Hoo's party.

"There is something funny about this,"
said Frisky, who was very wise for his
age. "I wonder who else has been asked."

So he went round
to find out, and
when he heard that
Whiskers the Mouse,

Tailer the Rat,
Mowdie the Mole,
Soft Ears the Rabbit
and Singer the Nightingale
had been asked, he sat and
thought hard again.

At last he took his fountain-pen and wrote
to say that he would go.
Then he went round to all the others and
said that he would call for them on the
party night, and would they please be
ready before the moon was up.

"But why?" they asked. "Hoo Hoo doesn't
want us till the moon is shining."
"Never mind," said Frisky. "You do as I
tell you, and you will be glad afterwards."

So on the party night everyone was ready
before the moon was up. The woods were
all in darkness, and Frisky went quietly
round to Whiskers, Tailer, Soft Ears,
Singer and Mowdie.

"We will all go to the hollow
tree and peep inside it to
see what Hoo Hoo the Owl
has got for the party,"
said Frisky.

"But we won't go by the front way. I know
a little hole at the back, and we will peep
in there, so that Hoo Hoo won't see us."

So they all set off together, and they
didn't make a scrap of noise. Soon they
came to the hollow tree, and Frisky led
them round to the little hole at the back,
and they all peeped through.

Just then the moon came up, and the little guests could see inside quite plainly.

And to their very great astonishment there was nothing to eat at all! Not a single thing! There was a big dish, quite empty, and five empty plates.

"Good gracious!"
whispered Mowdie.
"This is a funny
sort of party!"

"Where are all the
cakes and jellies
and things?"
"Shh!" said Frisky.
"Can't you hear
someone coming?"

The animals all listened and looked. And
whatever do you think they saw?
Why, Hoo Hoo the Owl coming into the hollow
tree with four of his friends, all owls
like himself!

"Sit down," he said. "Our dinner will be here soon. We have only got to wait! I do hope you'll enjoy the party."

The owls all sat down and waited. The little creatures outside hardly dared to breathe. They suddenly knew what the dinner was! It was themselves!

Then one by one they crept away to their homes. Whiskers went to his hole,

Tailer went to his.

Soft Ears scampered to his burrow,

and Singer flew to her bush.

Mowdie went to his nest,

and only Frisky was left.

He wasn't afraid of Hoo Hoo, and he kept
his eye to the hole in the tree to see

what would happen. The owls waited and
waited and waited, but of course their
dinner didn't come. It had all gone home
long ago!

Then the four owls flew at
Hoo-hoo in a rage and
pecked him hard till
he hooted in fright.

Then out of the hollow tree they flew in
a temper and left Hoo Hoo by himself.

Then Frisky called out cheekily:
"How did your party go, Hoo Hoo?
Did you have a nice time?"

He didn't wait for Hoo Hoo to answer, not
he! He fled up to the top of the tree and
hid there in safety, chuckling to himself
to think how angry the owl would be.
So he was – and he never gave a party again
in all his life!